Parents and Caregivers,

Stone Arch Readers are designed to provide enjoyable reading experiences, as well as opportunities to develop vocabulary, literacy skills, and comprehension. Here are a few ways to support your beginning reader:

- Talk with your child about the ideas addressed in the story.

- Discuss each illustration, mentioning the characters, where they are, and what they are doing.

- Read with expression, pointing to each word. You may want to read the whole story through and then revisit parts of the story to ensure that the meanings of words or phrases are understood.

- Talk about why the character did what he or she did and what your child would do in that situation.

- Help your child connect with characters and events in the story.

Remember, reading with your child should be fun, not forced. Each moment spent reading with your child is a priceless investment in his or her literacy life.

Gail Saunders-Smith, Ph.D.

STONE ARCH READERS

are published by Stone Arch Books
A Capstone Imprint
1710 Roe Crest Drive
North Mankato, Minnesota 56003
www.capstonepub.com

Library of Congress Cataloging-in-Publication Data
   Meister, Cari.
   The brave puffer fish / by Cari Meister; illustrated by Steve Harpster.
   p. cm. — (Stone Arch readers. Ocean tales)
   Summary: Everything scares Hardy the puffer fish, but when he is threatened
by a shark, he finds a way to be brave.
   ISBN 978-1-4342-3198-7 (library binding)
   ISBN 978-1-4342-3389-9 (paperback)
   [1. Puffers (Fish)—Fiction. 2. Fishes—Fiction. 3. Sharks—Fiction.
4. Fear—Fiction. 5. Courage—Fiction.] I. Harpster, Steve, ill. II. Title.
PZ7.M515916Bp 2011
[E]—dc22

                              2011000297

Art Director: Kay Fraser
Designer: Emily Harris
Production Specialist: Michelle Biedscheid

Reading Consultants:

Gail Saunders-Smith, Ph.D.
Melinda Melton Crow, M.Ed.
Laurie K. Holland, Media Specialist

Printed in the United States of America.
   012019   001466

THE BRAVE PUFFER FISH

by Cari Meister

illustrated by Steve Harpster

STONE ARCH BOOKS

a capstone imprint

HARDY THE PUFFER FISH

PUFFER FISH FUN FACTS

- The puffer fish is also known as the porcupine fish, globefish, and blowfish.

- When it is puffed up, the puffer swims just half as fast as normal.

- Some puffer fish can change colors to hide themselves. Others can change according to mood or surroundings.

- Some puffer fish are served as a special food in Japan. Because it is poisonous, chefs must do special training to learn how to cook it.

When Mrs. Puffy had a baby boy, she called him Hardy. The name Hardy means brave.

Mrs. Puffy told her baby, "The
ocean is full of hungry, fast fish.
Puffer fish are slow swimmers.
You will not be able to swim
away from danger. You will
need to be brave."

As he grew, Hardy tried to be brave, but it was hard.

"How can I live up to my
name?" asked Hardy. "The sea
is so scary."

Most of the time Hardy stayed home. He felt safe there.

When Hardy did go out, he always seemed to puff up. He got scared, sucked in water, and blew up like a balloon.

The other reef fish laughed.

"I'm not going to hurt you," said Trina. "Save your puffing for the sharks."

But Hardy couldn't help it.

Everything seemed to scare Hardy. The shadow of a boat spooked him.

Something shiny on the ocean floor startled him.

He even puffed up if another
fish swam by.

Poor Hardy. Puffing was no
fun. He could hardly swim
when he was big and bloated.

His tiny fins could not make him move forward. He just had to float on the ocean's current.

The other fish pointed their fins at him.

"There goes the floating ball!" they teased. "Maybe we should play catch with him."

"What happens if we poke him with a stick? Will he pop?" someone shouted.

"Don't be so scared all the time," Trina said. "You're one of the most poisonous fish in the sea. You don't have anything to worry about."

"Yes, I am very poisonous,"
said Hardy. "If something tried
to eat me, it would die. But I
would die, too."

One day, a shark visited the
reef. All the fish swam and hid.

But Hardy couldn't swim
away to hide. He wasn't fast
enough.

"I can't puff up," he thought.
"She would see me for sure. How
could she miss a big, bright
floating ball?"

"I know what to do!" said
Hardy. Then he changed his
color to match the sea grass.

The shark swam closer and closer.

Soon the shark was inches away. Hardy could count her teeth.

All the other fish watched from
their hiding places. Now they
were the ones who were scared.

The shark did not see Hardy.
She swam away.

When the shark left, the other
fish came out from hiding.
"Nice work, Hardy," they said.
"You were great."

Hardy smiled. "Thank you," he said.

And for the first time ever, Hardy felt brave.

The End

STORY WORDS

bloated

current

poisonous

puffer fish

reef

Total Word Count: 420

WHO ELSE IS SWIMMING IN THE OCEAN?